The
Angel
Babies XII
God of Dreams

CLIVE ALANDO TAYLOR

authorHOUSE®

AuthorHouse™ UK
1663 Liberty Drive
Bloomington, IN 47403 USA
www.authorhouse.co.uk
Phone: 0800.197.4150

Published by AuthorHouse 11/09/2017

ISBN: 978-1-5462-8454-3 (sc)
ISBN: 978-1-5462-8470-3 (e)

Print information available on the last page.

God of Dreams

INSPIRIT* ASPIRE* ESPRIT* INSPIRE*

Because of the things that have first become proclaimed within the spirit, and then translated in the soul, in order for the body to then become alive and responsive or to aspire, or to be inspired, if only then for the body to become a vessel, or a catalyst, or indeed an instrument of will, with which first the living spirit that gave life to it, along with the merits and the meaning of life, and the instruction and the interpretation of life, is simply to understand that the relationship between the spirit and the soul, are also the one living embodiment with which all things are one, and become connected and interwoven by creating, or causing what we can come to call, or refer to as the essence, or the cradle, or the fabric of life, which is in itself part physical and part spirit.

And so it is, that we are all brought in being, along with this primordial and spiritual birth, and along with this the presence or the origins of the spirit, which is also the fabric and the nurturer of the soul with which the body can be formed, albeit that by human standards, this act of nature however natural, can now take place through the act of procreation or consummation, and so it is with regard to this living spirit that we are also upon our natural and physical birth, given a name and a number, inasmuch that we represent, or become identified by a color, or upon our created formation and distinction of identity, we become recognized by our individuality.

But concerning the Angels, it has always been of an interest to me how their very conception, or existence, or origin from nature and imagination, could have become formed and brought into being, as overtime I have heard several stories of how with the event of the first creation of man, that upon this event, that all the Angels were made to accept and to serve in God's creation of man, and that man was permitted to give command to these Angels in the event of his life, and the trials of his life which were to be mastered, but within this godly decree and narrative, we also see that there was all but one Angel that either disagreed or disapproved with, not only the creation of man, but also with the formation of this covenant between God and man, and that all but one Angel was Satan, who was somewhat displeased with God's creation of man, and in by doing so would not succumb or show respect or demonstrate servility or humility toward man or mankind.

As overtime it was also revealed to me, that with the creation of the Angels, that it was also much to their advantage as it was to ours, for the Angels themselves to adhere to this role and to serve in the best interest of man's endeavors upon the face of the earth, as long as man himself could demonstrate and become of a will and a nature to practice his faith with a spirit, and a soul, and a body that would become attuned to a godly or godlike nature, and in by doing so, and in by believing so, that all of his needs would be met with accordingly.

And so this perspective brings me to question my own faith and ideas about the concept and the ideology of Angels, insomuch so that I needed to address and to explore my own minds revelation, and to investigate that which I was told or at least that which I thought I knew concerning the Angels along with the juxtaposition that if Satan along with those Angels opposed to serving God's creation of man, and of those that did indeed seek to serve and to favor God's creation and to meet with the merits, and the dreams, and the aspirations of man, that could indeed cause us all to be at the mercy and the subjection of an externally influential and internal spiritual struggle or spiritual warfare, not only with ourselves, but also with our primordial and spiritual identity.

And also because of our own conceptual reasoning and comprehension beyond this event, is that we almost find ourselves astonished into believing that this idea of rights over our mortal souls or being, must have begun or started long ago, or at least long before any of us were even souls inhabiting our physical bodies here as a living presence upon the face of the earth, and such is this constructed dilemma behind our beliefs or identities, or the fact that the names, or the numbers that we have all been given, or that have at least become assigned to us, is simply because of the fact that we have all been born into the physical world.

As even I in my attempts, to try to come to terms with the very idea of how nature and creation could allow so many of us to question this reason of totality, if only for me to present to you the story of the Angel Babies, if only to understand, or to restore if your faith along with mine, back into the realms of mankind and humanity, as I have also come to reflect in my own approach and understanding of this narrative between God and Satan and the Angels, that also in recognizing that they all have the power to influence and to subject us to, as well as to direct mankind and humanity, either to our best or worst possibilities, if only then to challenge our primordial spiritual origin within the confines of our own lifestyles, and practices and beliefs, as if in our own efforts and practices that we are all each and every one of us, in subjection or at least examples and products of both good and bad influences.

Which is also why that in our spiritual nature, that we often call out to these heavenly and external Angelic forces to approach us, and to heal us, and to bless us spiritually, which is, or has to be made to become a necessity, especially when there is a humane need for us to call out for the assistance, and the welfare, and the benefit of our own souls, and our own bodies to be aided or administered too, or indeed for the proper gifts to be bestowed upon us, to empower us in such a way, that we can receive guidance and make affirmations through the proper will and conduct of a satisfactory lesson learnt albeit through this practical application and understanding, if only to attain spiritual and fruitful lives.

As it is simply by recognizing that we are, or at some point or another in our lives, have always somewhat been open, or subject to the interpretations of spiritual warfare by reason of definition, in that Satan's interpretation of creation is something somewhat of contempt, in that God should do away with, or even destroy creation, but as much as Satan can only prove to tempt, or to provoke God into this reckoning, it is only simply by inadvertently influencing the concepts, or the ideologies of man, that of which whom God has also created to be creators, that man through his trials of life could also be deemed to be seen in Satan's view, that somehow God had failed in this act of creation, and that Satan who is also just an Angel, could somehow convince God of ending creation, as Satan himself cannot, nor does not possess the power to stop or to end creation, which of course is only in the hands of the creator.

And so this brings me back to the Angels, and of those that are in favor of either serving, or saving mankind from his own end and destruction, albeit that we are caught up in a primordial spiritual fight, that we are all engaged in, or by reason of definition born into, and so it is only by our choices that we ultimately pay for our sacrifice, or believe in our rights to life, inasmuch that we are all lifted up to our greatest effort or design, if we can learn to demonstrate and to accept our humanity in a way that regards and reflects our greater desire or need, to be something more than what we choose to believe is only in the hands of God the creator or indeed a spirit in the sky.

It was very much my intention not to state the name of any particular place in the script as I thought that the telling of the story of the Angel Babies is in itself about believing in who you are, and also about facing up to your fears. The Angel Babies is also set loosely in accordance with the foretelling of the Bibles Revelations.

I thought it would be best to take this approach, as the writing of the script is also about the Who, What, Where, When, How and Why scenario that we all often deal with in our ongoing existence. It would also not be fair to myself or to anyone else who has read the Angel Babies to not acknowledge this line of questioning, for instance, who are we? What are we doing here? Where did we come from? And when will our true purpose be known? And how do we fulfil our true potential to better ourselves and others, the point of which are the statements that I am also making in the Angel Babies and about Angels in particular,

Is that if we reach far into our minds we still wonder, where did the Angels come from and what is their place in this world. I know sometimes that we all wish and pray for the miracle of life to reveal itself but the answer to this mystery truly lives within us and around us, I only hope that you will find the Angel Babies an interesting narrative and exciting story as I have had in bringing it to life, after all there could be an Angel Baby being born right now.

After these things I looked and behold a door standing open in Heaven and the first voice which I heard was like a (Trumpet!) speaking with me saying come up here and I will show you things which must take place after this.

Immediately I was in the spirit and behold a throne set in Heaven and one sat on the throne and he who sat there was like a Jasper and a Sardius Stone in appearance, And there was a Rainbow around, In appearance like an Emerald.

Time is neither here or there, it is a time in between time as it is the beginning and yet the end of time. This is a story of the Alpha and the Omega, the first and the last and yet as we enter into this revelation, we begin to witness the birth of the Angel Babies a time of heavenly conception when dying Angels gave birth to Angelic children who were born to represent the order of the new world. The names of these Angel Babies remained unknown but they carried the Seal of their fathers written on their foreheads, and in all it totalled one hundred and forty four thousand Angels and this is the story of one of them.

Angelus Domini

God of Dreams 1

In being readily prepared to be born and then born again, never was there once nothing, as everything once was, as in the beginning there was no beginning, as everything once was and always will be so, and so as to find everything in a constant state of constant change and impermanence, fluctuations, and tremors, a slight effect of waves or wobbles, and yet as it is, that everything would stop and then begin to start all over again, withstanding that which had also invariably happened once before, and then again and again and again, as much before the true existence of nature itself, and much before it had decidedly been recorded by the instruments of earth, as to whether this infinite possibility were somehow that everything was occurring and also reoccurring at will, and yet as to whether time would lapse and rewind and reignite and then readjust itself accordingly, or even upon these fluctuations, that would result in just sending out waves and ripples of an aftershock or perpetual event, causing minimal adjustments to take effect, perhaps every one thousandth of a milliseconds, or a centisecond, or even between every one thousand four hundred, and every two thousand five hundred years, as in any time line or evolving event, would prove to be a subject within itself, in that everything was just naturally and progressively influenced or updated accordingly by such natural influence, but as to the true will or desire, or even towards the perpetual motion of time itself, was somehow that this recycling or reverberating and echoing event of all constituent parts, is a consistent and a constant anomaly, either disassembling or even reassembling and rearranging and adapting itself at will throughout the ages of all time.

As within the limitless possibilities and fluidity of time, however measured by such mechanical innovative technologies, would also support these ideas of life's theory, that life itself is too short to prove, or too long or to compare, to come about with a theory of such a big bang occurring once and only once, as this occurrence within itself would have to keep on happening and happening and repeating and reoccurring over and over again for time to even selectively be called or recognized and identified as time.

If somehow it was that what man calls God, could also described as a significant being, however supernatural or alien to the creation of humans, in having the abilities to adapt and influence and change at will any eventuality or circumstance, just by existing and also by allowing all other unearthly materials and substances to also manifest and exist alongside, as such are the preponderances of all living anima in bearing souls, and yet each having and bearing the primal ability to change and adapt and utilize all earthly materials and substances, as such is the inanimate object given energy and brought alive towards it sole purpose of existing, forever and however long it might take to fulfill its completion.

As also to attribute God a name, is to also investigate as to whom God is perfectly addressing, and for what person is any or all influence or instruction given, and also as to inquire as to why and where and when this revelation took place, and from where upon the face of creation did God appear to reveal such influential declarations to a single subject, as man is also and has always been the subject of influences and initiation within this the greater scheme of all life taking shape and having and bearing his or her own influences of will over it, so upon this examination, man is an influential tool, in having and bearing great propensity within his or her direct connection and relationship with God.

As for the idea behind the endlessness of any beginning, then let it be known and understood, that the same occurrence did not and does not happen twice in the same way, as in all inevitability and with any update or reinvention, is also to adapt and to change without exception but not as an exact copy or replacement of any, or all animate objects that exist, as in any upgrade or modification suggests that any event, and upon every repetitive change which has taken place or shape, so by definition is not the same beginning occurring effectively more than once and yet in a slightly different way, however exceptionally unique and different, these causes from origin may perpetually occur throughout the ages of all time.

If one is dealing with the future, then one is also viewing and dealing with the past, and yet one is also researching and examining the beginnings of the origins, but just suppose that the origins are beyond this earthly realm, and that all originality actually takes it root within the vast expanses of space and time, much before the very first stars and seeds of creation are born, as if for one aspectual reason, that creation takes on many forms away from the physical matter of the terra firma, and actually exists and multiplies itself into other substances as of yet unfamiliar to the past and yet uncovered in the future by this very revelation of time, as if the resources that we seek are to be discovered in different forms, then is it not, that this origin should also be caused to change and adapt and to evolve and take on new forms by the same effects of space and time.

Angelus Domini

God of Dreams 2

So how long does a day last if not twelve hours, and yet how long is a night if not twelve hours, and yet how long does it take for God to issue forth one day and one night, or should we first seek to understand that upon this first event and succession, that one day and one night was more than just a millennia and yet issued forth upon a single breath, and yet if God had ordained it upon several breaths, then would not several millennia succeed in going forward upon every event if only for the first time, and yet further still, if there was a second time or a second event, then would that not suggest to encourage or bring about another day and night, and so in bringing forth another seven more breaths for another seven more millennia, would that not be the beginning or at least cause the ushering inevitability of bringing future outcomes, as of yet untouched and unoccupied by human nature.

Even if the universe was actively mechanical as a perfectly tuned machine that readjusted and effectively functioned independently of any intervention, and also what then if the days and nights were followed by the regulatory influences of their own respective time of the seasons, as much as we have four seasons, well what if according to the realms of God, that these seasons were in fact ages of an era, spread across the ages of man's ability to learn and to adjust and to develop and to modify and to pilot itself towards the inevitability of a future that was in fact succeeding itself in perpetual motion, and perhaps according to the seasons of God's will and not that of the earth, but in active accordance with it.

For even the idea or the suggestion that the wheels of the Ophanim did stop and ceases to turn, then does not everything that is dependent upon the mechanics of the universe to function and flow with precision and fluidity also cease in its functioning, that is to say that everything stops except the nature of God, for how else can God influence his creation when all things are awake and functional, even though when we are wide awake, how many is it that is amongst us, that have witnessed God's intervention, especially at such and upon a critical time, so as to direct mans will towards a new millennia, or even to offset the beginning of a new era within an enhanced and enlightened perspective of his own will.

Of all the souls that are asleep within the sea of the souls, of all the lives that are plucked from existence, of all the promises that are buried unlocked within this guiding principle of everlasting life, surely it is a new day and a new age and a new chapter and new event that would arise to awaken their restful and peaceful residing souls, and are there not also other states of being and existences, such as spiritual as opposed to corporeal body, and surely there are other realms as opposed to earthly ones, set against the principle of the metaphysical, as much as we must aim to fulfill every aspect of this exploration of the different dimensions attributed to us as living beings, with or without the forming and appearance of a physical form, as it is only the earth that requires the retention of the physical form, and yet the soul must dwell within the seas of the soul, and the spirit must existence within the heavenly spheres of this creation, and yet upon Its birth and renewal, does not the resurrected body require a soul to dwell within it, and does not the spirit return after going to and fro between the heavenly realms upon its visitations, reignite itself within the reunited soul and that of the earthly body, as such is the holy spirit, and the body of the father and the soul of the son becoming in complete harmony with itself.

And so even as the earth becomes still, and the Ophanim ceases to turn, and the earth is caste into darkness, and yet in its entirety it is completely covered and protected by the celestial and empyrean forces, as it is neither day upon night, nor night upon day, as the dream of the Angel Babies is at long last, causing the formation of the earth to become renewed, and yet beyond this magnitude, mankind remains asleep, as if the universe were to become reborn and renewed out of the things that had preceded and gone before it, and yet what does God create beyond and outside of this unearthly substance and of what materials, and of what matter does God choose to renew and realign the manner of all things, and to what effect and design does God manifest the properties of all constituent and living beings, and with what attribute does God go about his creation, before setting all things once again into the fluidity of motion.

I mean imagine if we all went back in time, then naturally we would all return to our mother's womb and our father's seed, as our mothers and fathers would return back to theirs, or at least until time would effectively return back to the womb of the universe, and to the one singularity that ignited everything, but who is there to say, or to announce that we are indeed returning back to the womb of the universe, as much as we do not fully know what our mothers and fathers experienced much before we were born unto them, as there was a time and a period of time, that we did not exist to unto them, and yet how is it that when we are born, that we recall so many more things about the world around us than we could possibly account for, or even know and yet we are full engaged and aware of something so profoundly spiritual which most certainly affects and influences us in so many ways much before we even begin to realize and examine the true nature of it, as it seems even before conception, we were still somewhat connected to God and the universe.

Angelus Domini

God of Dreams 3

As the age of darkness had fallen over the earth, and all but the Angels were asleep, and as of yet had not descended upon the face of it, but remained steadfast and suspended high above the earth's stratosphere, casting their presence across the globe, very much like an eclipse emitting very little particles of rays of light very faintly through, that penetrated or broke through their lines and rankings of formation, and yet all that stood before them and the terra firma that we call earth, was the one lowly single sentinel, Angelus E'nocturnus who had dwelled and waited for the earth to become active and alive and revived within the fullness of its glory.

Of all the sounds resounding throughout the universe, the first remark uttered was first made by Proarkhe the Arke, in directly addressing Angelus E'nocturnus, in saying E' Nocturnālis, come up here, for you are the last of our kind, but upon his response Nocturnus expressed his concerns, for what of the earth in its final hour, and how can It be ended and deserted in such a dire way, the earth will not become extinct as you may have been led to think or believe, but what of Satan and the others who were fallen, are they not to be considered in this final bargaining, be warned and be aware Nocturnus, for Satan is no more, as this is but the last opportunity for you to become redeemed upon this the final act of this judgment, but look upon the earth now, does she not blossom in coming forth as I move across it, nay it is unfortunate and not so Nocturnus that you feel for the earth, then who else is dying within this act of finality, the only thing sustaining her heart beating bosom is you E'nocturnus, then send more Angels to assist in her healing Proarkhe, nay Nocturnus it is written and therefore must be done, as you alone cannot save her from this judgment, as it is God's will, that the earth be laid bare in her desolation, but how so, surely Satan can rule her once again, nay Nocturnus it is not so, as Satan is divided and stricken for all time and eternity, as the earth is the lords and all bound up within her, then I will not give up, I shall remain steadfast in my pursuit, nay Nocturnus you shall not, you shall turn to stone and die if you choose to remain, now I urge you to come up here.

Then pray tell me Proarkhe if Satan is stricken, then who else stands in place of his presence, as it is written Nocturnus, that no one stands in the place of his presence except the Archangel Lucifer, Lucifer! But I don't understand, how can It be that Satan is stricken and yet Lucifer is not, have you not already decided your own fate Nocturnus in trying to maintain and retrieve that which is irretrievable, then so it is that all things have returned to their primal origin, and so too has Lucifer been reconciled back to his primal origin, as I have said unto you that the earth and all therein are the components and the attributes of the Lord, but why has the Lord allowed for such a woeful and calamitous event to take place, because it is the end of days Nocturnus, and there is nothing that can be done to change it, as all that stand in the way of the earth's judgment is you, and you alone cannot change the will of it Nocturnus, so sayeth I Proarkhe the Arke, now become summonsed or become bind up and destroyed for the hindering demon that you are.

Of all the sounds resounding throughout the universe, the second remark uttered was that of Bythos the Aeon in directly addressing Angelus E'nocturnus in saying that the depth or profundity of this message is given over to you with a great depth of insight and knowledge, as you are aware that God so loved the earth that he sacrificed his only begotten son, so that the earth could through his stead would continue to go on and flourish, and yet through the deception and trickery and deceitful nature of Satan, that the earth and all of the things dwelling within it have become corrupted, as Satan was divided in that he insisted and persisted for God to do away with this creation, and in by doing so, end and his love of man, as Satan has only desired that God would hold him up in the highest of esteem, so that he alone would seek to have favor over all the dominions of the Angels in the celestial and empyreans, so now you see the profundity of this profundity that has become beset upon us all, But if God made such a sacrifice so that this world might be saved, then why has the Lord allowed for this to now transpire if Satan as you say is defeated, yes it is true because of this bargaining and reckoning that the earth has been brought to such a calamitous and graven decline and end, as you must now accept Nocturnus, that this is the reason for it and none other, now it is left to you to decide if you shall choose beyond the certainty or this reason to become reconciled and brought back unto this kingdom of heaven, but if I am to return unto the empyreans, then how shall I know what shall become of my fate and even that of the earth.

E'nocturnus Angelus, is it not true to say that you are an invaluable component and attribute unto the heavens itself, in that we should recognize that you are of a unique composition in bearing much ability to become useful and mutable upon the darkness's that rotate upon the earth, and is it not true to say that you have the ability to assist in the weaving and unto the whispering of souls within the depths and the mysteries of men within their dreaming, well yes suppose these things are notably true to say the least, but how can I manifest myself if no one is alive or even free to dream of such ethereal thing's of beauty, awe and wonder, nay Nocturnus, it is not us but God who behoves it, that you should be sustained in your deliberations of deliverance, that you should once again take flight and accompany the never ending evenings unto the dead of the night and ignite the dreams of the living even while they sleep, but what God in heaven requires an Angel of the underworld to perform such a task when there are no such subjects to attend too, the subjects are now and have become that of the Angel Babies Nocturnus, and the God of which you speak, is the God of Dreams.

Of all the sounds resounding throughout the universe the third remark was uttered by that of Monad the One, in saying Nocturnus, do you accept the unacceptable task and renounce the earth and accept God's will in that you shall now be summonsed or become as they say no more, but of course the terms are of an unacceptable oath, but If I accept them what shall be required of an Angel of my description and talents and means of merit, let it be known Nocturnus that if you accept these unacceptable terms, then you shall be granted the title of the oneness of the essence of exactly one hundred and twelve thousand legions of Angels, but if you reject these unacceptable terms then, yes I understand Monad, then I shall be extinguished and terminated, but what if I take charge of my new found redemption, is God so certain and willing so as to risk and sacrifice such a large legions of Angels for the use of my personal virtue and command, if not for the benefit and wit of my imagination, yes Nocturnus, but should you choose to defy God, then let it be known that you Angelus E'nocturnus did so choose to destroy the earth for the sole purpose and benefit to become ruler over of its earthly dominion, but that is an untruth and detestable statement, yes, but it may also prove to be true if you lament and go back on your choice of word in this agreement, then pray tell and instruct me as to how this act shall transpire between us Monad.

Angelus Domini

God of Dreams 4

According to the will of this command, so it shall be, that that one hundred and twelve thousand legions of Angels at the behest of God, shall there by enter into and dwell upon the earth by way of the Angel E'nocturnus, who's transformative embodiment shall become that of their own spiritual being and inhabitancies, but Monad wait, for if I agree to become the sole embodiment of such a legion, then by what means shall it be done, and what shall be my seal to prove it, and who shall be the guardian and caretaker of the earth in the absence of my presence, E'nocturnus, of all these questions, there are no consequences or worries of concern as they shall all be addressed and answered in time, but as for the time being, you shall be granted and allowed safe passage through these formations and rankings until you have succeeded to come before the Ophanim and throne of God, well then Monad, so as it is written then so let it be done, that I Angelus E' Nocturnālis did indeed upon returning to the celestial and angelic empyreans, did so willingly, and for the integral reason and purpose of not as you say in becoming reconciled, but in order to commit to serve the true and principle act of the oneness of essence, which should be fulfilled and met with upon this accord, and upon this accord alone, but tell me Monad, do you not have some reservation or trepidation of dread and fear of this power now being presented to me, if I am to indeed wield it, nay Nocturnus I do not, as I am aware that you shall no doubt revel within this act of impunity, but upon your consent and for any other reason in defining your own fate, just remember Nocturnus, that you shall also be responsible for one hundred and twelve thousand others in your keep and command, who may one day hold you to task or even contempt, should you choose to risk or jeopardize this undertaking, very well then Monad I shall agree to these terms, and now, if I am still welcome, I shall accept your invitation to come up as you say.

Within It's abandonment nothing moved across the face of the earth, as if creation itself was scratched and blotted out like a lifeless and limp fossil buried beneath its own historical decaying remains, and yet for how long the Angels remained positioned high above the earth's atmospheric dust, still remained unknown, as the ascent of Angelus E'nocturnus had begun to take flight, somewhat struggling to find form and stealth towards becoming airborne from the stony deserted grounds below, surrounded by a cold and harrowing and yet unforgiving and deafening silence, with none left to shed a tear or to scream outwardly beyond the why and the wherefore of such a trial and judgment that had now come to pass.

And now E'nocturnus, is it not true to say that you are relieved of the drudgery of this world, relieved, but how can I be relieved from this judgment, unearthed and plucked like a stone once rooted and embedded within a graveyard of forgotten souls, as of yet, not dead or deceased, but is not the earth polluted with God's of one form or another, of each and every description, then tell me this Proarkhe and Bythos and Monad, if the earth is polluted with God's of one form or shape to another, then are they not all cut from the same endless cloth of each and every description, in hypnotizing and possessing the souls of men as idol deities, and does not the fickle man flutter from one God to another, to fulfill his every whim and desire, if only to become a God himself, whether it be the metamorphosis of Morpheus or the warmongering of Ares, or the love of Eros or even the might of Zeus.

And who is this God of dreams, and is it not invisible, and are we not all said to be within the clutches, and the grasp of this oneness of essence, and moreover can this also be the same ancient one who is said to be the God of Abraham, or Isaac, or even Jacob and Moses, and are there not also other fishes in the seas to contend with that are not yet two of a kind, and yet who shall remain to be seen as the God of all, or perhaps even he is just as the seasons that solemnly come and go as all the other Gods seemingly do, nay Nocturnus, I bid you not to speak out of turn or error within this contemptuous nature, as it is this God that also posses the ability to summon and bind demons from an alternate plane to do his bidding upon any request of ambition, as it is always in dreams that we fly, as there is also truth to be found in these dreams, truth, what truth, when all around is us is the evidence of nothing but empty vessels strewn upon the rocks of desolation, or does this dreaming God ever wake up to find this evidence of a nightmare now an abandoned Eden, first you must free yourself Nocturnus, and liberate yourself, and emancipate yourself, for you were never the architect of this creation, as much as you have invested more than your time and efforts in order to secure and retain its salvation, as it is not the earth that is lost, but you my friend, so now let us go out and beyond this place, and seek out such a perfection besides the throne of this imagination, as all these things must come to an end, in order for all other such things to precedence and stand to begin again.

Of all the journeys ever made could it be, that the most significant one, is the one that takes place within, in causing us to look internally upon the face of reflections, focusing upon the change and metamorphoses, in stimulating a determinate will, if only to examine and to improve and to adapt upon what once was, and to then dig deeper and further into the subconscious levels and realms of self interrogations, if only then to then face the challenges and the struggles of a past, where once battles were fought within, for where is it written that an Angel is a winged demon or indeed that a demon is a winged Angel, when both are seemingly at opposite ends of the same spectrum, as such is the fallen now risen and vice versa, as even all of our souls are torn between these two polarizations, of damned if we do and damned if we don't, and yet the devil is in the detail, or further still, the devil may care, and in by doing so, may care not, and yet why is the earth, this precious earth, so valuable to all contenders and adversaries alike, and why is it for so long that the wars of one and all, have never been brought or resolved upon any cessation and conclusive reasoning, and so therefore put beyond any shadow of a doubt, that in coming face to face with the demon within, that what we actually find and discover the Angel of peace forever dreaming, and yet to awaken from a restful and peaceful reality.

As I have said that there are many sides to those of us who are actors within this story, as even as a coin that is tossed into the air has only two sides of which to land upon, then so also do all of the beliefs of this world also speak of the hell's and the heaven's which are between us, as it is also within these realms of which we are all actors dreaming, and yet even in truth we are also experiencing such reality's from time to time, from one end of the spectrum to the other, as such are the varying degrees and pathways between damnation and salvation, and yet within this story of change and transition are we not tempted by the desires of this world, set apart from the promises of a paradise, as it is the earth that is portrayed as the lowest level within these realms of our existences, set against the heavens as being the highest level of our achievements or attainments, which have now been found to be somehow embedded within psyche of our beliefs, and yet to die for it is surely to perish, or even to succeed in obtaining it, somehow begets an everlasting life, and so it is this acceptance of the unacceptable that determines the fate and will and desires of one and all, the oneness of essence.

Angelus Domini

God of Dreams 5

But tell me Pablo Establo Estebhan Augustus Diablo, the Immortal One, what would have happened if we were indeed foes, well then I suppose we would have to think very carefully about that, so what you undoubtedly mean is that we would have to anticipate each other's actions, like chess pieces, well I was thinking more like adversary's perhaps, well yes, but who would be the one forced to make the first move, would it be me as the challenger or even perhaps you as the defender, now listen to me Nocturnālis, as I have never slept nor missed a single battle within my timeline, so does this somehow make you feel like you are a superior Immortal, as I myself have also seen the instruments of warfare, conjured up and crafted by man's own imaginings, and I could quite easily impale you upon the bluntest and simplest of objects, but what makes you so sure that I can so easily be overpowered, well perhaps you are more of an observer than a participant actively engaged in the art of fighting, and perhaps you are just a silent witness to the methods and the madness enlisted in the art of war, a sacrificial pawn upon the chessboard of life, well then tell me more of this chessboard Immortal One, but there is nothing of which to tell Nocturnus, nay Pablo as I do believe that there is, I mean after all, who are you mostly likely to send first into the forum, and are we not all proven to be sacrificial objects amongst these so called pieces, nay Nocturnus, it is not so, as I am well aware and of any strike and counterstrike much before any move has been made, but tell me Pablo, if not the Pawn, then what about the Knight, don't you think that perhaps the Knight is more advantageous in determining and bringing about a victory, a Knight, or do you mean the night, where once the battles fought upon this earthly chessboard did indeed find and leave you defeated, the Knight, or a creature of the night, scouring the earth for souls to invade and influence.

Look Angelus E' Nocturnālis, it is high time that you woke up to the reality, that it is the force behind the throne, which is the determinate will of all, that shall decide the fate of the earth, as you and I are of an age old time, where long ago battles were fought over good and bad and right and wrong, where the fate of the earth was left for men to decide but not now, as such a time has come to expire, and what shall it benefit you now to know and to learn of these corruptible insights, that make these men the creatures that they are, and what can I do if I am to take stock and study man in his many complex ways, if only to see if he leans to the left or the right of his own achievements in advancing towards Godliness, and for what purpose or reason does heaven or hell require another war to vanquish all foes, towards gaining a complete totalitarian authority over such dominions, and how shall it be fought, if not between two singular polarized forces, or indeed between two armies, of one cast out, set against one of whom remains steadfastly held within the highest esteems of creation, yes the war is won and yet all else is lost, as who amongst us can bare to live within this old age, knowing full well, and in remembering the sacrifices given by all for their all, and yet for all of this greatnesses, is now found to be consumed and yet still considered upon this final day of judgment, or could it be that the Knight prays to the Day, and that the Day delivers the Night.

But is it not true to say Pablo, that even you in your place and stead having already experienced this subconscious feeling of déjà vu", then is it not then also true to say that God's rationale, is also one that is born out of an emotional attachment to this world, irrespective of any logical or practical progression towards it, or is it even truer to say, that this God of Dreams, is also a God of Death, nay Nocturnālis, tis not true to say it, as much God is often provoked into action upon such an accord, so as satisfy and yet to also diminish for whatever purpose and pleasure of will may determine it to be so, and yet are not all things still maintained in their own composition, if not for his love of this world.

Then tell me this much, as to why all things should die just to satisfy this truth of truths, have we not always been such loyal subjects according to the Cross of this sacrificial test, or is all such defiance and disobedience, to be brought back unto this earth, in order for it to judged and redeemed, and refined for the purpose of it, nay Enocturnalis, tis not so as it is only within the order of this oneness of essence, that all originality should actually become fulfilled, as life and death are simply said to be such extremity's between waking and sleeping, but surely if you fear to sleep, then perhaps you will never truly awaken, as you must be aware Angelus E'nocturnus, that the same thing may never happen twice again in the same way as much as it is continuously happening right now, so at all times you must be aware of your transitioning, from period to period and from time to time, as we may forget how easy it is a forfeit in trading places, if we do not stand firm upon the hourglass of shifting sands.

And so before you proceed any further, then perhaps you should ask yourself this question E'nocturnus, is it better to take from God or to give in his services, and is it better to ask of God anything, or is it better to act for his purposes, and is it better to receive from God, or to become as his vessel, a beacon and instrumental vehicle, of valuable transportation, acting in accordance within the will of assurances of his many varied and complex ways, as there is no journey placed before us without a true destination ahead.

As it is the prethought that precedes the beginning of the breath, and yet it is this breath that begets action, as much we are found to be speaking without thinking and looking without seeing, but to dream a dream inside a dream, is to see God's kingdom within with your eyes closed, but alas it was not always so, and yet as much as we have to think to remember, of that, of which we thought we knew, and yet maybe it was not so, or perhaps we did not take fully into account the influences around us, as even the energy that is also supportive of these elements also give their contribution to what defines us, as it is the will that becomes the force of action, and yet where is this will, if all action is stemmed from it, and if so, then are not all things arising witnessed from the forethought, and then does not all thought beget its energy from its own independent action, as much as we can only give an account, of that which we can contain, but as for the external matter, well it seems that we hardly ever notice the slightest of influences, or changes or adaptations along the way, even if only for an instance, and yet we have already thought of everything, and yet nothing has happened to redirect or even change the energy or elements around us, as such it is, that all things are still transient and in constant motion, but what do we see, and what can we feel, and what do we know except nothing besides ourselves, and so the thought that we are wasting time lingers, never really knowing if time is wasted after all, and so when do we actually become the thoughts that we think, or the words that we speak, and when do we choose to decide upon which side to stand, or upon which one to forsake, as much as it is shrouded in mystery, still I declare this God to you.

As which one of us has the time to watch a blade of grass blowing in the wind, or the patience to watch the ice turn into water, or vice versa, or even for a flower to spring forth from out of the ground, even though soon enough you shall come to realize that it is an unpreventable measure, and yet we take for granted the simplest of objects in our creation, as if they were simply of mere insignificance, but they are not, as you shall come to find, that they are even more important than you or I, in by giving us a greater awareness and responsibility of ourselves, that despite these objects of which all are made to interact, that in spite of their bewildering science, do we still not marvel at their naturalness, as you must heed the warning E'nocturnus, that I am not presenting God to you as a commodity, but as one who notices these mysteries within it, as it tis' but a God of love who is forever dreaming, and not the idol chess pieces of Kings and Queens and Presidents and Prime Ministers dreaming of new ways with which to fashion and rule the world.

Then tell me Pablo, what can happen beyond this point of watch for such an Angel, oh well my friend, I suppose that anything can happen in so many various ways, as each one are all found to be very peculiar, and yes we are all different in our aspectual ways, as there is no real definition of what you were or will be, as everything is so finely tuned, in that it's properties are so unique and individual, but what of fallen angels, were we not all once of the same composition, well yes I believe that you and I are of one substance, except that you have decidedly chosen to speculate and manipulate a darker degree of matter, so inherently, there is much that I suppose you are unaware, albeit a forfeit of something more virtuous and invaluable, so you mean to tell me that even one such I can become transformed, accepting that of repentance and forgiveness, but for what manner of interpretations are such confessions and begotten transgressions pardoned, believe me E'nocturnus, as even all faults and defects of uselessness's are transformed and treated accordingly within this translation, but firstly you must accept change within yourself.

Do we think to breathe, or do we breathe to think, for what is more important, and what is more natural, do we die to live, or live to die, for what is living if not dying, and why fear dying, when we did not think about it before the first breath, and who is the creator of dreams, and who forever shall be the dreamer of it, for if the first dream is the last dream, and as of yet the only dream, then are we not prepared for dreams as much as dreams come true, raining down from heaven like a thousand sighs of relief upon the thought of breathlessness, think not of the past E'nocturnus but only of the prominent role in this present, as your only true fear, was that the earth would be caused to be lost when it was not yours to lose, so therefore I shall meditate upon your praying soul, as I have nothing further to mention of these Godly matters displayed upon the wings of those favored, as it is time for you to transcend once again and above and beyond.

Angelus Domini

God of Dreams 6

Is it true to say that we can fly in dreams, and is it also true to say that there is truth in dreams, and if possible can we fly if the skies above indeed honor our true place amongst the stars, as the angels that lingered above, did indeed partly break the coordinates of their formation, in allowing for a brief moment in time, by giving way along the ecliptic plane, in allowing for Angelus E' Nocturnālis to ascend along the terrestrial equator, in order to guide himself through and out into space, whilst being under the gravitational effects of other celestial bodies of an elemental nature, as once he had succeeded their orbital paths, so too did they quickly react to close their ranks, in resuming and maintaining their positioning and realigning their formation whilst remaining suspended over the earth.

As Angelus E'nocturnus entered within the midst of the empyreans, he was quickly followed and met with upon this accord by those of whom had sustained and remained thereabouts, and yet they had become fascinated by this new arrival now being ushered forwardly and towards and now found to be in and amongst them, and yet as it was that these aspiring sentinels of a lesser degree were eager to inquire and hear and to acquire the news of a first account, from such a one as he that had witnessed upon this succession of such extreme events, but pray tell us Nocturnus, and give us insights into having lived and dwelt upon the earth for so long, and what of man and the men of which you have known and encountered can you tell us, as we have heard many things, well.

Well my little cherubs, concerning your inquisitive nature's, Man in his learning has strange and unfamiliar ways, as man is easily influenced by angels and demons alike, as man is not yet an angel and yet more than an animal, as man is somewhere betwixt them both, as man wishes more than he prays, and dreams more than he can achieve, and wants more than he can obtain, and yes it is true to say that I have affected men in their many ways of slumber and dreaming and also within their hopeful idleness's, but why did you interfere with man Nocturnus, why, because he called out to me in his desperation upon the dead of night, but why should you answer him, why, and why not, for it is better to know them by their many ways and behaviors than to not know them at all, and tell us Nocturnus, has man affected you also, yes of course, it is true to say that man has affected everything that he has come across and of what has come across him.

In remembering the earth and the history of this earth, is to recall the event of man throughout the ages as of yet filled with conquest upon conquest and yet failure upon disaster, while trying as a never-ending cycle, and yet not realizing of what is to be maintained within these infinite cycles of endless possibilities, and why does man prevail to triumph over all things, he does this simply to become the master of his own fate, and to what cost and point of purpose are such achievements to be accredited, well for all the wars fought, and for all of the trials, if not for all of the endeavors and pursuits to be achieved, but what is the purpose of man, if only to love and to build and to create and to challenge and to overcome and to strive and to pursue, and to innovate and to pioneer for his own pleasure and desire, for his own abilities to be admired and adored and recognized, both in and upon his own account, much through the poverty of his long suffering and the sickness, and the mortality of his advancements, but what is the purpose of man, his purpose is to tell his story to the world itself, in prayer and meditation and in thanksgiving and worship and through acceptance and kindness and goodness, and through the appreciation of the sacrifices made by this same relationship between man and other men, as it is also this story that is the beginning of the beginning and yet the threads of the end.

As in coming forward to approach Angelus E'nocturnus did one Noble Angel appear from out of the vast expanses of the surrounding heavens, that is Pablo Establo Augustus Estebhan Diablo, the Immortal One, are you friend or foe, well for now, as I have been summonsed here albeit for a better judgment, well I suppose that I am friend, and you are, I am the Immortal One, Pablo, and you are E'nocturnus, yes I am he, I have heard many thing's and seemingly passed you on by on many occasions, but if so Pablo, then why did you not acknowledge me upon my chosen pathways, well I did not because I could not, for the crossing of our paths at such a time would not have succeeded us up until now, so you suggest to indicate that it may have resulted in misadventure perhaps, well yes and perhaps not, but you are and have always being mentioned as being of a transient and mystical nature, so you do know me, yes but tell me E'nocturnus, how is it possible that one soul can withstand the judgments of the earth alone, well I do not know, except that only God can possibly answer this question, I see that you are unsure of this certainty, well perhaps you already know the answer to such a mysterious question Immortal One, all I know or even ever knew was time E'nocturnus, time for everything and time for nothing all at once, so you have never slept Pablo, no, no, not for an eternity, and what about dreams, have you not dreamt them, nay I have not, but I have seen what the outcomes of dreams have become in the fulfillment of reality, so you know the difference between the dream and their realities, yes I do, but how can this be so if you have not slept, it is because I have seen it across the ages, that when men wake up, that they immediately begin to live out this reality of their dreams, yes it is true that men do such a thing, so tell me, do you know your beginning, what do you mean.

Well what I mean to say is, do you know when all things began, well I suppose I don't recollect every minute detail, as I have dwelt within the underworld for so long, but why do you ask this question if the past is no more, I ask myself this many, many times, and I always forget to remember, that it all began in darkness, and that it also all happened simultaneously, as everything happened all at once, and kept happening, and keeps on happening, but funnily enough, it was always different in so many illusionistic and indescribable ways, except of course the absolute, the absolute what, well before you succeeded in coming here, the last one was a girl, a human girl, brought back from the brink of destruction, saved by one like you, Angel Ruen, so if he was like me, then what became of him, well I suppose he is now redeemed and with the others, what others, of whom do you speak Pablo, I speak only of those in the readiness and preparedness of Nejeru, so the world was prepared for this reason to become desolate after this child of man and woman, nay E'nocturnus, the earth is not lost, the only thing that is lost is you, as for the first rider, the second rider is coming, and for the second rider, the third rider is coming, and for the third rider, the fourth rider is coming and so forth, so that the revelation could become fulfilled and complete, so you speak of the apocalypse and the four horsemen, nay Nocturnus it is now ended, as it was always just the beginning of the end for all of our origins, and so for whatever reason and for what may happen, well no one truly knows, except perhaps you or God, but I do not know by which means of practices that you imply such suggestions, well I suppose neither do I Nocturnālis, but you must be here with us for some other reason or purpose don't you think, yes things are strange to say the least, as I am aware that I am to present myself before the Ophanim and throne of God, yes things are strange and unfamiliar, so perhaps this is the time for God to act.

And what of the earth when you finally left her, the earth was not left blossoming but dark and cold, for the darkness's had left her freezing and calling out for warmth like an endless winter, and yet there was still a faint voice inside of her, a voice between the heart and the mind that whispered in my soul, yes I also know this voice, as many angels have heard it, but very little have responded or acted upon it, except now, as there is also another voice that has taken shape deep within her place, and I now know that it is the voice of the lord, and it speaks with such volume, full of conviction and awe and wonder, and yet it is surprising to me how familiar it is, like a direct channel of communication between the spirit and the soul, yes I have heard this voice also, and by surprise I have also reacted to it with great affections and immediacy, as it cannot and must not be ignored, except Nocturnus, you must try to marry all four corners of these attributes before the Ophanim and throne of God, as the heart is the soul and the mind is the spirit, and yet all together they are also the oneness of essence.

Angelus Domini

God of Dreams 7

But wait Pablo Establo Estebhan Augustus Diablo, from where do you go to now, such expressions of dreaded fear and despair, but I'm afraid Angelus E' Nocturnālis, to tell you that I go to nowhere, for this is my home and by will of rights dwelling place, but look ahead, not with doubt but with hope and joy, for behold her now as she comes to lead you by the way, that you must henceforth and go, the Celestial Angelic Angel of the Aura, shall take you there, as by no other means can your journeying be sustained, you look surprised and yet somewhat confused, well that is to say that I am my Aura, well of you I can also say the same demon, but you seem somewhat disapproved of me, well I suppose I am, although it is not my place or position to be in judgment of you, except that I am, as this unfortunate occurrence is the only way for you to become approved upon such an administering of gifts, as it have never ever been sanctioned that I should perform such a task upon one such as you, but what of Angel Ruen, is he not one such as I, don't toy with me demon, as I believe that you have never before graced such inexpendable heights within the halls and corridors of creation, nay that is true to say that I have not, but why so accusatory if you do not know of my deeds within these myths Aura, a demon with wings is all I see before me, but look again Aura, as I also carry the burdens of hope, yes I am aware of such hope, as this is the reason why you we're not smitten, good, well I suppose I should be thankful for your understandings, thank me not, for I do what I must do, as you should also do demon.

It seems that you would pour scorn upon a lowly soul, well I suppose that you are a lowly specimen, but am I not destined for great things Aura, according to the Immortal One, I shall be improved, Improved! you say, well yes it seems that within your hopes, perhaps there is some room to shed some light, but you are still a wretch, and I am only here so as to perform such a task so as to give you what you need, in knowing full well that you possess a valuable talent no doubt into the ways of men, who I believe, are also wretched creatures, yes it is true to say that I am blessed in knowing such ways of men, a blessing you say, or more of a curse, as I do not even wish, or to seek to know such ways, but why so my Aura, as man is not so bad, well if you say man is not as you say he is, then why else has one so lowly as you been summonsed here in the aftermath of such extremities, ah yes, well I see your point in this position, well perhaps I shall be the cause of change upon this matter, and perhaps you shall not, but be the cause of stirring up even more erroneous subjects, nay my Aura, it is not so, then how is it, it shall be a time of great chance and changes, very well then, be silent, for I shall bestow upon you the Halo of the celestial angelic aura, but as to whether it can be fitted and attributed to you, well we shall soon remain to see.

As the Halo was about to be placed upon the head of Angelus E' Nocturnālis, for a moment he became hesitant and apprehensive, wait a minute my Aura, as I not quite sure for what I am destined, but could you at least reassure and confirm with me that I am not now dreaming or perhaps even worst still, caught up in a never ending mystery from which I am certain to never wake, tis but the lucidity of clarity that requires such a reality to never truly reveal itself as true or untrue, as even in dreams there is truth but what else could be so is real, now be still wretched demon, as this shall indeed redirect your senses towards the inevitability of your future examination, as it was that the halo was now put and placed upon the head of Angelus E'nocturnus, who's imperfections were now perfectly retuned and realigned so as to begin his ascent towards the place of the Archangel, much beyond the empyreans, do you feel it Nocturnus, yes I do Aura, and do you know it Nocturnus, yes I do Aura, then fly towards the will of this command, as you must now go this way alone without my further influences or guidance.

How can one know the thoughts and the feelings of God's own instinctual core, and how can one taste the ambrosia and the nectar of such essence, and become consumed by all manner of things, from the source of all purities, for what does this enduring God think, and by what force of actions is he caused to move, and upon what energies of sustenance does he feed, and from what fields and vineyards does he quench his undying thirst, or is true to say that perhaps he is in need of nothing, nothing but empty vessels, so as to fill them all up with all matters of boundlessness energies, poured forth from an overwhelming fountain of unlimited and immeasurable love, for if it we're not for this love to be levied and sacrificed away as an instrument of the heart and the mind and the soul of spiritual embodiment, born of the same cosmic dust and ashes, filled to the brim and bursting forward, reigning forth with truth and justice upon its armor, a never ending promise of promises.

Aura tell me unconditionally, do these Angels love their God, as a child clings to its mothers breast for milk, and does this God also chasten and display such moralistic behavior as a father is taught to discipline his children, and does this God reward these angels for their merits of conduct, as much as a child is praised for its abiding efforts, and yet if this structured habitat is built and erected astride the back of Angels, whether it be a shelter for celestial and empyreans alike, then what of the stranger within the midst of such a household, if this be the home to one and all sentinels, then what of these heavens to an outsider and living creature, damned to hell beneath this place, held in contempt like an organism wanting and needing to survive, or can it be that this breath of life is simply left to die once it has become expelled from the body of the father, and yet it cannot not truly die if the peacemaker is at war with himself, for therein lies the fate of one and all, if not to be at peace besides oneself, knowing and in honoring the light of wisdom, which comes to satisfy every piece and part of this fragmented creation.

And what of the navigational amazement of such an Halo, redirecting the will and engaging the senses, in causing one's own nature and thoughts to become attuned and clarified, for whatever I myself thought I was, well perhaps I am not, and in rooting out all sicknesses and corruptions of resistance, as once more I becoming a part of the whole complete subject, but is this trial also a conditional one of obligatory necessity, that in possessing such an instrument of will, that I have now discovered and become aware besides myself, or in identifying that unbelievably so, that I was once was at odds with the inner workings of my former self, and yet in realizing now that I am becoming transformed and enlightened by being in possession of such a simple gift of virtue.

Angelus Domini

God of Dreams 8

If it were not for such a great burden of responsibility, of unimaginable expectations now lifted, and not yet granted, then how else could I have known what was required of me as to where this Halo would guide or lead me too, for how else could I have known, that as I had now arrived upon the edge of a swirling black hole, somewhere out of reach, and positioned much beyond the shimmering sparkling stars that group together, in recognizing and knowing, and mystically tying themselves together, invisibly joined and connected as one and all, to the tree that is life, as it was upon entering this event horizon, now twisting and spiraling through a mass of darkness, that I begun to see the world rotate and fold in and upon itself fluidly and quite randomly, without conscious effort or systematic order, as if the beginning were not the end but the midway, and as if the midway were not the end, but somehow the beginning, and also as if somehow this beginning were somehow regenerating and mapping itself out of newly formed elements, jumbled up, and yet becoming redefined through a prism of distorted repetitious cycles of all and yet any and every event, as it did even send tremors that caused ripples of time to profoundly impact upon me, like a heartfelt emotional chain reaction from which I could not fathom all.

As I began to emerge from being spun around and ejected from this void of darkness, that still it seemed to me, as if nothing had changed to influence such an outcome, or was it, that I was still to be denied and defeated upon my expectations of what appeared to be the other side of nowhere, as nothing had materialized or come forth to reveal itself to me, nor could I see any definition taking shape or form from out of this density of darkness that had fallen over everything, nor was there any kind of sound to know or to learn if something was hidden and lurking in the blackened depths, or could it be that I was to be deceived all along, so as to be foolishly led into this all consuming bottomless pit, now to be my all enduring prison of loneliness and despair, or perhaps this was the outcome of a living death, in not knowing if all eternity had closed its doors upon me, and so I pulled my knees towards my chest and wrapped my arms, as I folded my wings around me so as to cocoon myself from this embittered harshness surrounding, and upon closing my eyes, my only comfort in the dark was from my halo.

As it was then, that the faint voices and remnants of an age old unknown past began to haunt me from within,..Hark is that you,..Say that Haven sent you, but I am Zyxven,..Well listen and hear me well Haven, for I am Angel Ruen the first pronounced consummate Angelic Son of Ophlyn,..Angel Nephi of the Nephilim, thusly you are redeemed... Papiosa was a man seeking divine and infinite knowledge of the abode of the angels,..A creation of the celestial abode die,..But how can that be,..Then it is done, one day we shall eat fish together by the stream you spoke off and we shall save every mortal soul,..She knew not anything of justice, let her be,..For unbeknown to me in the present context of my conscious mind,..My father Angel Simeon did indeed appear but not to me as I would have wished,..But once it was written and recorded by Pablo Establo Estebhan Augustus Diablo the Immortal One, that in the book of the Unwritten Laws,..Do you know why in your adornments of the blessed Angel Aura that you have been summonsed.

By the time I had awoken and arisen from out of my meditative sleep, so it would seem that I had acquired the greater insights of some thirty two thousand angels, of those of whom I did not yet know, and yet such powers of their energies did surge through me, in causing a charge of knowledge to course through the very fabric of my inner being, in bringing about a greater understanding and awareness of those who come by this way before me, and yet I was still gripped by this uncertainty as to what I was to think, or to do, or even to pursue next from out of this all knowing and prevailing quickening of this reality, as even now their trials and the event's of their stories echoed and resounded throughout the inner thoughts of my mind, as if I were a part of them, or that somehow they had become a part of me, but as to why I was made to be visited by such a number of thirty two thousand strong, seem to me, to be partly connected to the reason that some kind of accounting was taking place, and that I was somehow the vessel chosen to contain such a record of these Godly accounts.

And so bemused was I in thinking to myself, as to what would happen if I were to repeat my previous my actions, in being suspended here in the middle of nowhere known or affirmed to me, and yet I could only hope to anticipate and to engage and to interact with any kind of form or formless entity which might offer me some form of insight, and so once again I closed my eyes, eagerly anticipating and watching and awaiting if any visitation should take effect again upon my being again, as I now became aware that perhaps I was now seeing things through the prism of an altered state, and yet upon each of these stages, I was visited upon in spirit, by a certain number of presences, that affected me in such a strange and peculiar way, as it was this cluster of stars in their numbering, that also hung within this place, and yet still they possessed the ability to influence me in such a way, so perfectly positioned within the state of their fixed illuminations, suspended around and about me, as it began to emerge and dawn upon me, that if it we're possible to create a world inside another world, or even perhaps to turn the world inside out and then somehow enter within, as much the birds that inhabited the skies, and fishes that inhabited the seas, and the animals that dwelt upon the land, worlds within a world, and yet by the slightest chance of circumstances, somehow, and for a moment in time, we had all traded our places, or could it simply be that God had ordained it, in trading positions with me.

As once again I had woken up from out of this state of dreams, and in gaining some insight as to what was taking place and effect upon me, and yet as soon as I had opened my eyes, there was a green gaseous mist all around me, like that of an aurora borealis, as I realized that within the midst of it stood seven angels, of which were unlike any other, in that they were revealed to me as the archangels, standing guard over what appeared to be the Ophanim, as it was upon this moment that Uriel, and the six others did approach to draw near to me, in saying Angelus E' Nocturnālis, you have slept and awoken, and now you are arisen, but for how long have I endured, and of what fate belies ahead of me, you must arise and take your place upon the Ophanim, yes I have heard of this place where every wheel turns, but tell me where are the number of stars of which I dreamt, speak Raphael, you have endured only a season E'nocturnus, a season, but by what measure, speak Michael, by the measure it takes to fulfill this dream, but you puzzle me archangel, speak Raguel, you are but one of a few E'nocturnus, who's abilities are exceptional, and you have majestically satisfied a great task, but what was the task, to sit idly alone and ponder the universe, speak Zerachiel, nay E'nocturnus, but to separate night from day, but what has happened since my dreaming it, and what of God, speak Gabriel, as it was so, then so shall it will be, as another season awaits you E'nocturnus, but for how long Gabriel can I endure this will, has not God put an end to all things, speak Remiel, did you not see what God has laid out before you, the oneness of essence, but what of the others, and the earth and the hundred and twelve thousand legions, and my seal, am I to be used as a pawn or a decimal point in separating one place from the next, speak Uriel, go in peace Angelus E'nocturnus, for you shall be granted more than you have accounted for in this bargaining, as it was at this juncture that the archangels directed me to Ophanim and the throne of God, in order for me to fulfill my summonsing.

Angelus Domini

God of Dreams 9

And yet if prayers were heard, then who has listened to them, and if prayers were answered, then who has fulfilled them, for if it were not for these Angels of these Heaven's, then for all we know about the soul, is that it becomes nothing more without a body, as even within this definition of the soul cages, given that they were held and contained, or even imprisoned synonymously, as the simplest of creatures, otherwise crustaceans, scouring upon the sea bed floor, shedding their skeletal forms in order to moult and grow, but as to whether they we're even aware that such a judgment had befallen upon them, or that they had once indeed, inhabited physical and upright bodies of flesh and blood.

And yet also, what about this spirit, and to where did it rise up and go to once it had ascended upwards towards this Heaven's, and for how long did it choose to remain there, for all eternity amongst these heavenly stars, or did it otherwise become purified and purged of all its ills and torments, whilst becoming cleansed and washed thoroughly through, in being suspended highly above, seated within the presence of God upon this Ophanim of such indivisible numbers, until such a phase of time would allow it to transcend and descend back into the bosom of the earth upon becoming a new being or creature.

And what of rebirth and rejuvenation upon this plane of metaphysics, if whereby their souls should meet and reignite with their infinite spirits once again, as much as before their entanglement, they were once also separate hosts, divided, and yet upon this oneness of essence, they are made to become joined together and manifest, and yet if they are born once again, then how shall it be if they are to take on a new form, and what now of these souls arising from out of the seas below, and what now of these spirits descending from the skies above, for is it not a necessary union and unification of all things, to begin to take shape and transpire in moving forward, and yet as if it were, that not all things brought forth are called unto the living of a new life, for no matter the words or the sounds being expressed or pronounced, the true nature of all the exchanges of the heart, is between God and the Spirit.

Once seated upon the Ophanim, I paused to think and imagine of what would take place and transpire next, as I was propelled and accelerated beyond this realm, with such a force of great immensity, and yet I knew that either I, or everything else as I had known it, would not be the same as it was before, as the grains of sands had shifted, but to what extraordinary degrees, well I did not know, and yet for the day and night to become separated, only suggested that the hands of time had ceased to advance and turn, which only reaffirmed to me, that somehow I Angelus E' Nocturnālis, was still to remain as a blackened pawn possessed in transit, somewhere between the middle of a darkened sky, set upon a path where dreams and nightmares begin to meet, and rest upon the wings of an underworld skilful Angel and forceful spirit such as I.

As not so much but when I arrived, I was to return to this place that is the sentinel abode of the celestial empypreans, except that once again much to my surprise, I was left dumbfounded in confusion, for I came across to see, that there was nothing there, nothing except the brightest glare of pure infinite white light, spreading out across this great expanse, so much so that it was blinding to my eyes, but equally I could feel the balances of all living anima, becoming restored naturally, as all that was contained in me was none other, than that of Angelus E'diurnālis, albeit a direct reflection of what my inner being possessed, and yet slowly and surely, one by one, the Orbs of one hundred and twelve thousand legions did proceed to surround and preside within me, and so it was that my gaze and transcendent focus, was now able to be brought back to look upon the earth all renewed and aglow, as everything had begun to return itself towards its' given composition, of both its beauty and bountifulness, as it once was throughout all eternity, as even I Angelus

E' Nocturnālis did began to realize the reality and the gravity of the dreams of God, as his graciousness fell upon me.

As it was from this point and position in time, that something was to become born from these abiding silences of transformation, as I felt much besides myself within this quiet and yet thoughtful presence, and yet so it was that I should be inclined to use my senses and intuitive perception, along within the mind's elusive art of conjuring and stimulating the vividness of my imagination, as there was no definition or detail that could describe that once was the separation of spaces, now soon to become occupied and inhabited by the multitudes, who had once lived within this metropolis, and yet as for when the heavens were made to come down and cover the earth, then so it was to be pronounced forth by the celestial empyreans, that this place Nejeru or otherwise this New Jerusalem, was for those who would come to claim this inheritance.

As over time it had come to be revered and known as the pillar, or the bedrock and stone of heaven, in being presented to us as a living thriving paradise, something spoken of as a sanctuary and a home to mankind alike, a romanticized place of splendor and love, and one that gravitates towards harmony, and peace of tranquility, in possessing complete compassion, as if encompassing all within its sanctuary, but what of this heaven unraveling like a thread of Avalon, and where do these mysteries and mysticisms end, in order for balance to restore itself upon these solid foundations, for as much as there are dreams, and as much as there is magic in the art of dreaming, as of this heaven, it is said to be both soft and subtle, and yet tender and fragile, and yet further still, it is fortified and solidly rooted within the foundations of the earth, and yet still found to be embedded with such beliefs, that appear to be full of such awe and beauty, as if said to be a remarkable transformation of the heavens itself.

For when the heavens did come down to greet us, still one heaven remained above us, and yet for the first time when the heavens opened up, still we were held by the suspense of our own imagination, in the infancy of wonders and expectations, and yet to explore these heavens, is to excel far beyond the reaches of a mystical xanadu, a place where the light of life breaks through the optical prism, casting all colors of all hues across the spectrum, as I do not doubt but abide with this hope and faith, as I begin to see that this place, a holy place of refuge and of quiet meditations, and a place of stillness and contentment, and a place of peace and quiet tranquility, and a place of change and transformation, and a place of reflection upon consolation, and a place of unity upon reconciliation, and a place of remembrance upon acceptance, and a thoughtful place of love and thankfulness, as it once was, and now is this heaven, Nejeru.

As to whether the sun was rising, or indeed if I was descending was of little consequence, as for this suspended moment in time, it did not matter, as now the heavens once again resounded proudly above, as did the restoration of the earth resound proudly below, as this was my endless prayer, which was one that was to be met with jubilation and exaltation, as this home away from the celestial empyreans, was the place that I was made to dwell, if only to weave in and out of hypnotic dreams, causing the anima to be affected endlessly, for what was now the dreams of the Angel babies, was now one for me to bear upon my Seal, In Somnis Avolaminus.

~*~

~*~

Printed in the United States
By Bookmasters